D1119237

Noodle, Nitwit, Numskull

by Meguido Zola

Illustrated by Jillian Hulme Gilliland

Quarry Press

JUL 3 0 2002

For Marah and her friends,
Amanda, Julie, Katie,
Lupine, and Pippa

THE WORLD

is full of *shlemiels* – noodles, nitwits, numskulls –
but the biggest *shlemiel* of all was surely Shlemiel himself,
who lived in a whole village of *shlemiels*, or fools.

Here are a few stories about this ninny, this nincompoop, this foolish
shmendrick and *shlimazl.* I tell these stories more or less as I recall hearing them,
as a child, from my grandfather the rabbi, the wandering scholar and storyteller ...
who in turn heard them from his grandmother and grandfather ...
who in turn heard them from ... and so on, and so on,
all of it just as it really happened to Shlemiel, long ago and far away,
among the Jewish people of mediaeval Europe.

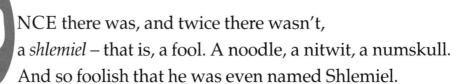NCE there was, and twice there wasn't,
a *shlemiel* – that is, a fool. A noodle, a nitwit, a numskull.
And so foolish that he was even named Shlemiel.
Forgetful, too. For instance, it was so hard for him to remember
where his clothes were when he woke up each morning, that he just
dreaded going to bed at night – just because of all the trouble he knew
he'd have when he got up!

Now, everyone tried to help Shlemiel, of course. But do you think
that was of any use? The very opposite! For every suggestion they came
up with was sillier than the one before, and more foolish than the next:

"Don't change when you go to bed!"

"Don't dress when you get up!"

"Don't go to bed!"

"Don't get up!"

And so on. And each solution made the problem worse ...
Until Shlemiel had an idea: to remember something, you tie a knot
around your finger, don't you? Or write yourself a note on the
back of your hand, right?

Well, Shlemiel would go one better.

"To find my clothes," he announced, "I'll take pencil and paper and, as I undress for bed, I'll write down exactly where I put everything. Everything. Exactly."
And that's just what Shlemiel did.

The next morning, pleased with himself, he took his list in hand and read: "Socks" – there they lay: he slipped them on.
"Hat" – there it was: he put it on his head. "Pants" – there they hung: he got into them. And so on, until he was fully dressed.

"There!" he cried out at last. "But... but ... now where
am I myself?" he wondered. "Where in the world am I?"
Well, he looked and he looked. But it was all for nothing.
Shlemiel could absolutely not find himself. Anywhere.

NE morning after breakfast, as Shlemiel daydreamed by his open kitchen window, he saw a stray hen and her chicks wander into his garden.

What a stroke of luck, he thought. Now I'll get rich and live in style! I'll catch the chicks and they'll grow up and lay eggs.

Then – guess what? – the eggs will hatch more chicks. The chicks will grow up and – yes, that's it exactly! – they'll hatch more chicks, that'll lay more eggs, that'll hatch more chicks ...

In time I'll sell out and, with all those big profits, I'll go into land.

I'll buy land cheaply and I'll sell it expensively.
This way I'll get more and more land. In time, I'll develop my land.
I'll build on it – houses, parks, shops, schools, synagogues,
and so on. Whole streets of them. Towns, cities.

Hundreds and thousands of workers will be at my beck and call,
while I take it easy and just give out orders.

"Hey! You good-for-nothing idlers!
Work harder or it'll be the end of you!"
Shlemiel hollered out of his window.
But at that sudden terrible noise,
the hen and her chicks took fright
and scattered in all directions.

And that was the end of Shlemiel's chicks and eggs,
Shlemiel's lands, Shlemiel's houses, parks,
shops, schools, and synagogues, and
Shlemiel's towns and cities.

ONE morning, Shlemiel and his friends were talking
about how to gather in more stocks of salt fish for
the coming winter. They decided to collect the salt fish
they already had, and to cast it all into the village pond: that way,
Shlemiel said, the fish would breed and multiply for the next season.

"I have white herring in red brine," said Shlemiel.

"I have smoked carp," said Shmendrick.

"And I have sardines pickled in tomato," said Shlimazl.

"Well, let's cast all the fish into the pond,
and we'll soon have a rich harvest."

And each family
threw their leftover fish into the pond.
When winter came, Shlemiel and his friends went
to the pond to replenish their fish. They fished and
fished, but they caught nothing save a great big water-eel.

"Imagine!" they exclaimed in horror. "This wicked eel has gone and
  eaten all our fish!"

"Yes! What shall we do with him?" roared Shlemiel.

"Wring his little neck!" shouted Shmendrick.

"Tear him to tiny pieces!" yelled Shlimazl.

"Shush, shush," said Shlemiel. "That would be too kind.
  Let's drown him in the pond instead."

So Shlemiel, Shmendrick, and Shlimazl threw the wicked water-eel into the pond to drown, and that was that.

 N market days, Shlemiel liked to ride his donkey into town; and he liked to ride together with his best friend, Shmendrick.

But Shlemiel had a problem: he could never tell whose donkey was whose.

So Shlemiel docked his donkey's tail. Now his donkey had a
short tail, his friend's had a long tail, and Shlemiel could at last
tell the two donkeys apart ...

Until one day his friend's donkey lost part of its
tail in an old fence.

So Shlemiel notched his donkey's
ear. Now his donkey had a
notched ear, his friend's didn't,
and Shlemiel could tell the two
donkeys apart again ...

Until one day his friend's
donkey nicked its ear
on a tree branch.

So Shlemiel measured the two donkeys:
"Aha!" he said to his friend, Shmendrick: "Looks like my black
donkey is a hand taller than your white
one. Now I'll have no trouble
telling them apart!"

NE day, Shlemiel got
all dressed up
and went to town.

About the middle of the day, Shlemiel's stomach began to grumble.
Shlemiel was famished.
He went to an eating-house.
He ordered a bowl of chicken soup and dumplings.
Slurp, slurp. Munch, munch.
He ate it all up. M-m-m! De-li-cious!

But Shlemiel was still ravenous.

So, he went back to the eating-house.
This time he ordered a plate of
chopped liver with onions.

Chomp, chomp. Munch, munch.
He ate it all up. M-m-m! De-li-cious!

But even then, Shlemiel was still ...
just a little hungry.

So ... back to the
eating-house he
went again. With his last
coin, he ordered the only
thing it's possible to get
for so little money – a
glass of hot water and half
a slice of sweet honeycake.

Slurp, chomp. Munch, munch. He
finished it all up. M-m-m! De-li-cious!

And guess what? He wasn't
hungry any more.

"Uh-oh ... but what a noodle I am!"
Shlemiel clapped his forehead.
"Oh, what a numskull, a nitwit,
a nincompoop ... wasting all my good
money like that. I should've just got
a glass of hot water and half a
slice of sweet honeycake in
the first place."

N his way home, Shlemiel went to the tailor's shop to buy new clothes for the Sabbath.

He saw a
fine black velvet coat:
"Hmmm ..." he said. "I like it."
He saw some shiny black silk pants.
"Hmmm ..." he said. "I love them."
The coat and the pants were the
same price. He asked to try them on.

Shlemiel tried on the pants, and walked up and down.
Then, he took them off and handed them back
to the tailor.
He tried on the coat, and walked up and down.
Then, he started walking out of the tailor's shop.

"Stop!" the tailor called out. "You haven't paid for the coat!"

"That's true," said Shlemiel, "but I left you the pants."

"But you haven`t paid for the pants, either," said the tailor.

"Well, I should think not!" said Shlemiel. "Why should I pay
  for something I don't want?"

MALASPINA UNIVERSITY-COL
LIBRARY

ONE afternoon, Shlemiel was at home working in his garden when he saw a wild turkey pecking at some seeds he'd planted. Shlemiel chased after the turkey with a stick. But the silly bird only flapped around in circles until it ran into a tree and knocked itself out.

That night, Shlemiel held a feast for his friends. It began with turkey pâté; it went on to turkey soup and dumplings, followed by turkey roast with all the trimmings; it ended with turkey savory pie.

Shlemiel could not get over how this turkey had got into his hands. From then on, with a big stick in his lap, he would wait on his doorstep watching for another turkey to wander into his garden.

Passers-by would call out: "Shlemiel! What on earth are you doing there?"

And Shlemiel would whisper: "Shh! I'm waiting for my supper."

Shlemiel waited and waited. But no turkey ever came.
People tried to explain to Shlemiel how God's wonders never come twice the same way. It didn't change Shlemiel's mind.

Since then, whenever people talk about someone expecting something that'll never happen, they say: "Shlemiel's waiting for his supper!"

Text copyright © Meguido Zola, 1990.

Illustrations copyright © Jillian Hulme Gilliland, 1990.

Design by Peter Dorn, RCA, FGDC

All rights reserved.

Canadian Cataloguing in Publication Data
Zola, Meguido, 1939-
Noodle, nitwit, numskull

(Silhouette folktales)
ISBN 0-919627-87-0 (bound). –
ISBN 0-919627-89-7 (pbk.)

1. Jews – Poland – Folklore – Juvenile literature.
2. Schlemiel – Juvenile literature. 3. Tales – Poland.
I. Gilliland, Jillian Hulme, 1943- . II. Title.
III. Series.
PS8599.062N66 1990   j398.2'089'9240438   C90-090162-4
PZ7. Z64No 1990

Published in Canada by Quarry Press, P.O. Box 1061, Kingston, Ontario K7L 4Y5

Distributed in Canada by the University of Toronto Press
5201 Dufferin Street, Downsview, Ontario M3H 5T8